I Forgive You

JACQUELINE E. PERRY

DENVER, COLORADO

This is a work of fiction. The events and characters described herein are imaginary and are not intended to refer to specific places or living persons. The opinions expressed in this manuscript are solely the opinions of the author and do not represent the opinions or thoughts of the publisher. The author has represented and warranted full ownership and/or legal right to publish all the materials in this book.

I Forgive You
Lies, Betrayal, Infidelity & Learning to Love Again
All Rights Reserved.
Copyright © 2013 Jacqueline E. Perry
v3.0

Cover Graphic Designer © 2013-Myrna Galan. All rights reserved - used with permission.

This book may not be reproduced, transmitted, or stored in whole or in part by any means, including graphic, electronic, or mechanical without the express written consent of the publisher except in the case of brief quotations embodied in critical articles and reviews.

Outskirts Press, Inc.
http://www.outskirtspress.com

ISBN: 978-1-4327-9791-1

Outskirts Press and the "OP" logo are trademarks belonging to Outskirts Press, Inc.

PRINTED IN THE UNITED STATES OF AMERICA

Acknowledgements

I would like to thank God for allowing me this opportunity to share my voice and talent with the world, giving me second chances day after day, and most of all, for forgiving me through all my mistakes, which I like to call "life's little lessons." I thank my family, especially my parents, Jasper and Elizabeth Perry for supporting me, loving me unconditionally and providing for me whenever I needed them. I thank my siblings, Torsha Smith and Tim James for showing support and believing in me and always looking out for my best interests.

Lastly, thanks to my friends, educators and colleagues who never doubted me, who believed in my dreams, who supported me, encouraged me, motivated me and always had my back no matter what.

Stephanie Elliot

Peace & Blessings

Stephanie Elliot

Peace & Blessing

Contents

1

The Marriage

Growing up as a teen in the early 1990s, Jordan began to experience firsthand the ups and downs of relationships with the opposite sex. Her junior year in high school was the moment she met her first love and encountered her first heartbreak, all in the same year. Still not experienced in dealing with emotional issues involving adult relationships, four years later, at 21, Jordan married. She met her husband, Tevin, during her sophomore year, while he was attending graduate school. Soon after, she dropped out of college and decided to focus more on her marriage. Putting her goals and dreams on hold, Jordan moved from her hometown of Huntsville, Alabama and moved to Stamford, Connecticut where her husband, ten years her senior, received a new job opportunity.

Little did Jordan know, a string of tragic events would begin to unfold in less than one year of her marriage. Her husband, Tevin earned a lucrative salary as an advertising executive for a top ad agency in New York. The stress from his job began to take a toll on him and the marriage. Jordan chose to live as a housewife and take care of things at home, and at the time, Tevin did not have a problem with that.

"Hi Honey," Jordan said.

"Yeah, Hey," Tevin said as he came through the doorway after a grueling 10-hour day at the office.

"Where's dinner?" Tevin said in an extremely intimidating tone. Jordan was no fan of cooking, and he refused to spend money on a house staff when Jordan was at home daily. "There's pasta and steamed veggies on the stove, Sweetie," Jordan told him.

"Where in the hell is the meat, Jordan, huh?" Tevin yelled. He threw the food on the kitchen floor and stormed out of the house. Jordan began to sob, and then started cleaning up the floor before the dog started to lick it up. "At least the darn dog appreciates it," she mumbled to herself.

Tevin didn't come home until around midnight. By that time Jordan had cried herself to sleep. The next morning, he left for work but not before telling Jordan, "I expect a real damn meal ready when I get home."

As the days passed, this behavior became routine and Jordan became accustomed to it. She had no job, no degree and felt that this was the only option—to stay in an unhealthy marriage—at least for now.

Tevin's behavior went from verbal abuse to physical abuse. Each time he hit her, he apologized with flowers and other very expensive gifts. The whole situation became portrayed as acceptable. Lying and pretending to family, friends and their church, became stressful for Jordan. They put on this act that fooled everyone except Jordan's mother. Every time her mother called, Tevin was never home and Jordan's explanations never sounded convincing. Her mother's suspicions did not fly well with Tevin—at all. But he kept quiet about it…for a little while. Jordan's mother began calling more often, certain that everything between her daughter and Tevin was not going well. "Why does your mom keep calling every single day? It's ridiculous," Tevin said in a demanding tone. "You are a grown woman and she treats you like a child. Keep our business between you and me."

"She's my mom, for goodness sake," Jordan said.

"Look!" yelled Tevin, "answer the phone again when she calls and see what happens." To keep as much peace in the household as possible, Jordan only talked to her mom during the day while he was at work. Tevin's controlling behavior continued to get worse. Not only did she have limited interaction with her mother and other family members, he ran off her friends with his rude attitude, and he controlled everything from the way she wore her hair to her style of clothing.

Jordan grew tired. She was absolutely miserable and wanted a better life—a healthier life. She felt that getting out and looking for a job might help ease the tension between her and Tevin. Although he liked being in control of every aspect of the marriage, Tevin was surprisingly fine with the idea of Jordan getting a job. Tevin ended up finding her a job a few months later at a local radio station where he had several business contacts. Jordan finally felt that she had a little bit of independence.

Tevin was not as violent; things seemed to be getting better, except for one thing—he was hardly ever home. Soon, it was like they had separate lives. Once she started making money, they paid bills separately, but Tevin even made her pay a portion of the mortgage. While Jordan was excited about her new-found independence, she no longer wanted to be in the marriage. For both their families' sakes, she felt that it was important to keep up a "good" image.

Jordan was in her third week at the radio station. She worked as a public relations assistant and enjoyed it. She started to become more encouraged about going back to school to finish her degree. She also enjoyed working with the people there and became particularly close to Dilan, vice president of marketing, to whom she reported. Dilan had worked there for about 15 years. They spent long hours working together on many projects and promotions. Jordan felt closeness with him, a closeness that she wished she had with her husband. Like Tevin, Dilan was also quite a bit older than Jordan. As months went by, the working relationship turned into a romance.

Every day, Jordan came home to an empty house. This only made her long for Dilan even more. One day, Dilan called Jordan into his office. At this point, the romance had begun to interfere with their jobs. Co-workers noticed Jordan in his office more often, saw them going to lunch daily, and giving little winks and smirks as they passed each other in the hallways. Jordan eased her way into Dilan's office. She

I FORGIVE YOU

began to give him a kiss but he pulled away. She looked at him, confused, and said, "What's the problem. Why are you acting like this?"

"Sweetheart, listen. We need to be careful. I think people are starting to talk," Dilan said softly.

"Okay, Okay,"

Jordan yelled. Dilan told her to lower her voice and began to remind her that she was still a married woman, confused, looking for love that she wasn't getting at home. Jordan didn't say a word. She stormed out of his office and went back to her desk.

At home, things were still distant between Tevin and Jordan. He came home when he felt like it. She spent most of her time alone in their five-bedroom house. Every day the tension increased. Tevin was always stressed from work. He would have drinks after work, then come home looking to start a fight. One night when Tevin was home talking to his mother on the phone--something he did often--he asked Jordan to pass the remote so he could turn the volume down to hear his mother.

"Okay, honey, just a minute," Jordan said with a slight attitude in her voice. As soon as he got off the phone, he struck Jordan across the face and began to beat her with his fist repeatedly. She quickly ran downstairs to the kitchen and grabbed her cell phone and keys before he could hide them from her. She ran outside and drove off in her car. He got in his car and chased her. Jordan, now a nervous wreck, gave up and turned the car around and headed back home. Tevin grabbed her, hugging her and apologizing. "Baby, I'm sorry.

5

I'm so stressed with work and with this child support issue. I'm sorry, I'm sorry," he cried out.

While Tevin did work long hours and was fighting in court with his first wife, Jordan knew there was no excuse for his abusive behavior. Jordan just looked at him with disgust. Not saying a word, she quietly walked into the guest room, closed the door and cried herself to sleep.

The next morning, she awakened with flowers surrounding the bedroom and a handwritten note from Tevin that read: "I love you more than I love myself. Please forgive me." Attached to the note was a credit card. Jordan called her best friend, Mia, to tell her the whole story. "Girl, he has the nerve to think he can always buy his way out of anything," she told Mia.

Mia said, "Let's go shopping!" Jordan smiled but she was not up to it, as she did have a swollen and slightly bruised face. After ending her phone call with Mia, Jordan fell to her knees and began to pray. "Lord, please comfort me, guide me, and strengthen me. Have mercy on me, dear Lord. In your Son, Jesus' name, I pray. Amen." She got up and felt a sense of relief, knowing that everything would soon be okay. The weekend flew by; after Tevin left the flowers, note and credit card, he was gone the entire Saturday.

Dilan had been trying to reach Jordan and left a few text messages. Jordan ignored most of them but later decided to respond. He wanted to meet with her and discuss their little argument at the office a few days earlier. He told Jordan that although he was living as a single man, he was still technically married to his wife with no plans to divorce just yet; but he also realized that he was falling for Jordan. "Sweetie,

I wanna see you. Can you meet me at the park in about an hour?" Dilan asked.

"I don't know," said Jordan with hesitation. He begged her until she finally gave in. She knew that Tevin wouldn't be home for hours, if he came home at all. So she left to meet Dilan at a nearby park. As she entered the parking lot she noticed Dilan's car and parked next to it. She got out of her car and got into Dilan's car.

"Hi," she said.

He looked at her and gave her a long kiss. Jordan began to tell him about how Tevin had been treating her and that he recently hit her.

"You can't put up with that, Jordan. You really need to leave," Dilan told her.

"So why aren't you getting a divorce and why are we always meeting in places other than yours if you two are separated?" she asked.

"Babe, it's complicated, you know that," he said.

Jordan sighed.

"I'm moving into my own place in another week or so," he explained. The romance seemed to be progressing too fast in the short time she'd been working at the radio station.

"And I'm sorry for the blow up last week at the office. We just need to be careful. I don't want anyone suspecting anything. Now let's go to a hotel. I'll have a nice massage and spa day ready for you. Sound like a plan?" Dilan said.

"I don't know. He may come home early," Jordan mumbled. Dilan laughed and said, "Wow, does he ever?" Jordan began to open the door of the car and Dilan grabbed her by the arm and kissed her again, telling her how beautiful and special she was to him. Jordan smiled and said goodbye. As soon as she returned home, she checked the voicemail on the house phone, and found a message from Tevin saying that he loved her and would be home soon. It was 7:00 pm and the message was left around noon. Jordan sat on the sofa and relaxed before going to bed.

The next morning she got up to get ready for church. She noticed Tevin had not been in bed so she looked downstairs to see if he fell asleep on the sofa or in one of the guest rooms. Then she looked in the garage. His car was not there. She tried calling his cell phone and it kept going straight to voicemail. Tears came as she continued getting ready for church. She knew at that moment that she needed to leave him. When she arrived home from church, Tevin had left. Clothes were gone. All she could do was cry.

Months went by and Tevin continued to come in and out as he pleased even though he was renting an apartment close to his job. Jordan continued to see Dilan despite the guilt she carried since both of them were still married. Tevin wanted the marriage to work, but on his terms. He basically wanted to have his cake and eat it too. Jordan was sure that she wanted out and began to seriously think about moving out of the house with no plans to tell Tevin. Dilan, on the other hand, was no better when it came to commitment. He also wanted to play both sides. He continued to confess his love for Jordan, yet he was continuing to go back and forth to his wife and kids. Soon Jordan would find that she was not the only one he was supposedly in love with.

Each day at the radio station, Dilan and Jordan would give each other the goo-goo eyes and everyone in the office knew that something was up. They left for lunch every day at the same time, but in separate cars. Jordan was longing for that special love or what she perceived as love, a feeling she never got from her husband. The more she talked to Dilan, read his "love emails" and spent time with him, the closer her heart grew to him.

JACQUELINE E. PERRY

Imagine yourself as each character, what would you do differently in each circumstance?

What specific advice would you give to each?

What Bible verses would help Jordan get through her trials?

_____

_____

_____

_____

_____

_____

_____

_____

_____

_____

_____

_____

_____

_____

_____

_____

_____

_____

_____

_____

JACQUELINE E. PERRY

_____

_____

_____

_____

_____

_____

_____

_____

_____

_____

_____

_____

_____

_____

_____

_____

_____

_____

_____

_____

_____

_____

_____

_____

_____

_____

_____
_____
_____
_____
_____
_____
_____
_____
_____
_____
_____
_____
_____
_____
_____
_____
_____
_____
_____
_____
_____
_____
_____
_____
_____
_____

2

The Affair

Jordan began to think about the time she was spending with Dilan and how unbelievable it was that she felt so much passion for him. He told her, for the most part, everything she wanted to hear. But there were times when he seemed to feel that she was becoming too attached, so he made it clear that although he felt deep desire for her, it couldn't go any further; especially since he was back and forth with his wife, Linda.

August 1, 2002

Hi Jordan,

I have read your email several times trying to gain a better understanding of you and especially what you feel inside. I am very pleased to know that you have hope for a better life both in a spiritual and a worldly sense. It is especially pleasing to me that you have come to the realization that you must make yourself happy first and worry about others later.

Now as far as I am concerned and what my desires are as they concern you... I find you extremely attractive and I would love to make passionate love to you. However, I do have reservations because I know that deep down inside, it is more than a physical attraction. I realize that it cannot dwell too much on those feelings. Rather, know that it's safer for us both to focus on the physical aspects of our relationship even though we have not experienced that yet. (I am excited just thinking about it even as I write this.)

One thing I want you to know.....I am not an Angel...... never have been; never will be. But I am a nice person and I can say that I will never disrespect you or take advantage of you in any way. This is perhaps the reason I have not put any pressure on you about seeing me or trying to push you to the point where you are vulnerable to me sexually. I want you to want me as much as I want you....and I am a very patient person when it comes to what I want. However I can say I cannot wait until the moment I hold you in my arms and give you the pleasure you desire and deserve.

Dilan

JACQUELINE E. PERRY

August 5, 2002

Hello Jordan,

Reading your email made my heart skip a beat from over excitement. I never imagined that you were feeling that way so long ago. If I had known then, things would be a lot further along than they are right now. Making love to you is something that I have dreamed about so much. So when I get that opportunity, I hope that I can control all the passion that I feel for you.

I noticed the date and time that you wrote this email and it is very weird because I almost gave you a call. However, I talked myself out of it because I thought that maybe Tevin was with you. I guess I was wrong and I should have followed my first inclination. Anyway, there is nothing I can do about that now, but going forward I want to spend as much time with you this week as I can. Linda leaves on Tuesday night and will not be back until Sunday. So maybe I can get you to relax with me and we can enjoy each other.

Dilan

August 8, 2002

(Two days after Dilan and Jordan encountered their first moment of intimacy...)

Hello Jordan,

Yes, I was a bit nervous. I was nervous for a couple of reasons. First of all, I do not make it a habit to cheat, even though I have had my weak moments in the past. However I was more nervous because I was with you. I was with a person that I have a lot of respect and admiration for. I think you are one of the most beautiful and precious women that I know. In addition, you are sexy and modest; all the traits I like in a woman. All these things somewhat intimidate me.

The other night was a little less passionate than I imagined and I think it was because of nervousness. I also think it had a lot to do with it being our first time together in that way as well as it being your first time in the arms of someone else besides your husband. I was not sure if I could please you as you deserve and I was a little hesitant to completely let go. However, the night was still very wonderful for me and I think that it was wonderful for you as well. And I dearly would like to share more of these nights with you.

I find myself drifting away, thinking how lucky that I am to have you as a special friend. Making love to you the other night was not just for the fun of it or just for the sex. For me it was much more than the physical aspects of it. Jordan, I think that you are special.....I always have and always will. It bothers me that you think that you are "just another woman to have sex with." You have to think better of yourself even if no one else does.

Dilan

August 12, 2002

Jordan,

It pleases me that you think about me a lot because I think about you a lot as well. Saturday night was great even though it was brief. Sometimes brief is better than long periods, but with you brief seems like an eternity because I cherish your company.

By the way...did I tell you how beautiful you looked? I got excited as soon as you walked out of your door and when I called you back and you told me you were in your gown, my heart skipped a beat. Not to mention I wanted to come back and ravish your naked body.

They say you learn something new every day and Saturday night I learned something that I think will benefit us quite a bit. I learned that if I want to do it, just do it and do not ask. I wanted to make love to you so bad, but I did not want to cheat you or me with a quickie. I hope that you enjoyed your time with me and I am looking forward to spending even more time with you.

Dilan

The romance between Dilan and Jordan became intense. Months had gone by and Jordan finally moved out of the house. Of course, Tevin was not happy about that. She left one day while he was at work. Since he spent more time at his apartment, it was a few days before he realized that she was gone. One night when he came to the house, he noticed some of the furniture missing. He was in shock. He didn't know what to think—if the house had been burglarized or what. So as he walked through the house calling out Jordan's name, he began to call her cell phone. No answer. He called her parents. He called her sister…nothing. He kept calling and calling.

Jordan finally answered. "Yes, Tevin?"

"What in the hell is going on, Jordan?" Tevin yelled.

"Tevin, I've had enough and I've tried talking to you. You just won't listen. The marriage is over. You are rarely home and I'm fed up. I want a divorce," Jordan said.

Tevin's voice cracked as he begged her to come back home.

"Home? Do you really think that place is a home?" she said. Tevin continued begging her not to leave him. Later that night, Jordan decided to come over to talk. She drove over to the house, and Tevin was there waiting upstairs in the bedroom. He was sitting there with a glass of alcohol on the night stand, dressed in boxers and a t-shirt. He was already a little drunk by the time Jordan got there. Crying out to Jordan, Tevin kept shouting, "I want you back; I want my wife back. I'm so, so sorry." Jordan noticed the gun on the night stand and discreetly called 911.

"Tevin, Tevin!!! she yelled.

Tevin was hyperventilating. Jordan was in shock and didn't know how to console him. The police and ambulance arrived. She explained the situation and the paramedics checked his blood pressure and other vitals. Concerned for her safety, the police officer firmly asked if Jordan was ok. She told them that things would be fine. Tevin continued to sob and yell out, "I just want my wife back."

The police and paramedics finally left. The police temporarily took the gun into custody for the safety of both. Jordan ended up spending the night at the house. She had sex with Tevin, as emotionally painful as it was for her. While he was asleep, she sneaked out early the next morning. While driving to her new apartment, she began to pray and repeat a verse in the Bible. *Matthew 6:14-15 For if you forgive others their trespasses, your heavenly Father will also forgive you, (15) but if you do not forgive others their trespasses, neither will your Father forgive your trespasses.* Jordan arrived back to her place and stayed in bed most of the weekend, depressed. She took no calls and she had not informed friends or family, not even Dilan, of where she moved.

Back at work, things were a little quiet. Dilan, who travels quite a bit, was gone for the week. Jordan stepped outside to call Dilan and told him about her decision. "What? You moved out?" I hope it wasn't because of me, Jordan," Dilan said.

Jordan explained, "No, I've been thinking about this for the past year and finally got the courage to do it. But I do admit that since you came into the picture, it kind of pushed me to make that decision."

Jordan continued the conversation and began telling him of a time when she met him years earlier at an event and had fantasies of them being together. "Life seems to be full of bad timing, huh?" Jordan told Dilan. Dilan was a little busy and soon ended the conversation. Later that night, Jordan emailed Dilan.

August 13, 2002

Hi Dilan,

It's about 11p.m. and of course, I'm alone...I missed hearing your voice today. I hope you had a safe trip...and I wish you a safe trip next week. I guess I'll see you before you leave. I want to finish our conversation that we started last week! There are so many things that I want to share with you, but I know I can't give you my heart completely....Here I go...starting to cry again....

It's amazing how a simple gesture or a few kind words can make me feel so happy. I finally learned that material things cannot make you happy....(well...) Really, I mean that...I know that I can only make myself happy, but for me, it feels good when someone else shows that they care...I just hate feeling alone...I still don't understand how you contacted me (a few months ago) out of the blue. In some ways, I'm glad you did....and sometimes I wish you didn't, because I can't give you my heart...and that sucks! I guess I shouldn't think about it...But sometimes I think "What if...?"

JACQUELINE E. PERRY

I'm always creating these fantasies in my head...and I'm hoping that you will be in that fantasy...You always tell me how special I am, and how much you admire me..I hope that you can show that the next time we're together....When you hold me, when you kiss me, and when you make love to me...I want to feel your passion for me...I'm beginning to like you a little more than I did at first. You mentioned before that last week you were holding back or something like that...Why? I want to share some very intense, passionate moments with you....because that's all we can do...You have someone to go home to, and I don't....I have always come home to an "empty" house with no love or desire...

Well, since I have finally come to the realization that Tevin disrespects me and shows no love, I have given up on him...I am now focusing on my career goals...and besides that, I need affection, and right now you're the man that can give that to me...I don't feel guilty at all when it comes to Tevin..but as a woman, I feel bad for Linda...BUT...(there's always a but) It's not my fault that you stepped into my life when I really needed you...I can't wait to see you, Dilan...I really mean it!

Well, it's about 11:30...you're probably asleep...and I know you're not thinking of me, because you have someone else to think about...but I feel the same way you feel—You will always be a special friend to me...and whenever we end our "little romance"...I hope that we will still remain friends...

Hugs and Kisses,
Jordan

The next morning, Jordan checked her email. Dilan had responded:

August 14, 2002

Hi Jordan,

I miss your voice, but you know I'm busy travelling with little time to call you. But reading your email filled my heart with so much joy that if I had the choice of talking to you or getting a passionate email as this one, um-mmm, well, that's a "no brainer." Anyway you made my heart melt with your expression of passion and openness that I knew you had inside.

I am also pleased to see that you are realizing just what a beautiful and important person you are......not only to me, but others who care about you.

You expressed so much in your email that it really caught me off guard and many of your comments I will address when appropriate. The passion I feel for you....will definitely be expressed when the time comes....I will call you later.

Thinking of You Always,
Dilan

Although Jordan was separated from Tevin, she did begin to feel guilty about having a sexual relationship with Dilan--not only because she was still legally married but also because Dilan continued to show confusion about his marriage and exactly where he was headed in regard to staying in it or leaving.

As soon as Dilan returned from his trip out of state, he had to prepare for another trip, this time, out of the country.

August 15, 2002

Hi Sweetie,

Sorry to neglect you today, but I have been extremely busy trying to get everything done before I leave for Costa Rica next week. I hope that you are not mad at me....if you were it would break my heart.

Also, can you spare a few moments for me this evening.... say about 6:00? I'd like to see that beautiful face of yours so that I can have a pleasant night thinking how lucky I am having you as a special friend.

Thinking of You,
Dilan

Jordan was surprised that Dilan called her "Sweetie" and she told him that she wasn't sure about seeing him on that day. He emailed her back:

Yes you are my Sweetie....I must admit that I am starting to like you more and more. I have always known that you were special, but since I have gotten to know you better...I can definitely say that you are one of the most wonderful women that I've come in contact with.

By the way...I really love the way you feel in my arms. I hope that I pleased you the other week....because you pleased me more than I could have imagined. If I did not please you, believe me I will next time and the times after that. As I am writing this, I am getting excited.

Anyway...it is OK that I will not get to see you tonight... but the picture did the job. Now I can go home and dream about you.

Dilan

Things seemed to be getting so intense. The passionate emails made Jordan even more confused. Deep down, she wanted to obey her vows and stay married; but, on the other hand, she knew that the marriage was not healthy. She felt that Tevin would not change. Months went by, and Jordan struggled financially, even though she withdrew about $20,000 from one of the bank accounts that she and Tevin shared. At first he was furious about it, but he forgave her and just wanted her back. Tevin even said he would go to counseling for anger management. He was also willing to meet with their pastor. Jordan still felt that Tevin was not completely serious about the marriage. However, she agreed to attend counseling with him for several weeks. In the days following the sessions, he showed little initiative in winning her heart back. He continued to say that the marriage would only work if she would agree to his terms. He promised not to be abusive, but wanted to continue doing whatever he wanted to do as the man of the house. Jordan began to realize that the only reason he wanted to save the marriage was to keep up this fake image of a happy marriage for his parents and other family members back in his hometown, as well as friends and colleagues.

A month passed, and Jordan decided to see a divorce attorney. She wanted to weigh all of her options. She felt lost. Tevin had backed off from begging to save the marriage and changed the locks on the door and the codes to the gate, security alarm and garage. Dilan traveled more and didn't have much time to spend with Jordan. She began to gain weight and felt depressed; especially after she was laid off from the radio station. She blamed Dilan for the loss of the job because she felt he could have helped save the position. During Jordan's depression, she didn't socialize much at all, she didn't look for work, she didn't try going back to school, but she did pray daily. Prayer was the only thing that got her through this stage in her life. She didn't attend church that often, but always had a special bond with God. While she prayed, she also enjoyed reading Bible verses to help her get through the day. A few of her favorites were: Psalm 34:18, "The Lord is close to the brokenhearted and saves those who are crushed in spirit." Psalm 41:4: "O Lord, have mercy on me; heal me, for I have sinned against you."

Although Dilan was inconsistently in her life, he did help to pay bills while she was out of work. Whenever he wasn't travelling he would stop by and bring groceries or anything he could do to help Jordan during her darkest days yet. At 29, Jordan was learning to become independent for the first time. She was now just a few months short of her 30th birthday. Tevin had turned 40 and moved on with his life but constantly fought with Jordan regarding alimony and property they owned. With limited financial support from her family, Jordan could no longer afford an attorney and the money she withdrew from their shared savings account was soon depleted. For a long while, they put the divorce on hold and continued to live separate lives. Tevin began dating and later became serious with a successful restaurant franchise owner from Maryland. She was very sophisticated, well-polished and business-savvy--much different from Jordan, who was soft spoken and still "finding herself." Tevin was probably less likely to walk all over or abuse the new woman in his life; she appeared to be a no-nonsense type of woman.

When Jordan learned about this new relationship and heard rumors about how well he treated her, she was extremely disappointed. She was disgusted and felt humiliated. All she could think of was how unfair it was for her to experience a completely different side of him for several years. Rather than sulking in a deeper depression. Jordan wanted to get her life on track and start over. She went back to school and completed her degree. Then she started working toward her teacher certification. Dilan agreed to help pay for school and continued paying her bills. Jordan fell deeper in love with him, even though she rarely saw him. In her mind she felt that he indeed must have loved her dearly to show so much support and care. Why would he do all of these things for her if he didn't love her? In reality, he did a whole lot more than Tevin ever did as a husband.

Jordan was beginning to become more excited about her life now and the future. She emailed Dilan about all of her accomplishments and could not wait to see him again. She wanted to know where they stood in their relationship and whether or not he was truly separated from his wife with plans to divorce.

November 11, 2002

Hello Jordan,

I enjoyed reading this email because you opened up and shared your thoughts with me. It also pleased me because you seemed very confident in the things you were saying and you also showed the aggressiveness that you sometimes tend to hide. One thing you have to understand, rather should know about me, I was once a very timid person and everything seemed to pass me by because of it. When I see someone that is so much like me, I tend to want them to understand that they must not accept things but make things happen, especially in your case. When I see you, I see a very beautiful and talented woman that has a lot to offer the world, which is what made me fall for you the first time I saw you.

I hope your day goes well and I really miss you and I can not wait to hold you in my arms and look into those beautiful brown eyes of yours.

Dilan

Once they finally got the chance to see each other, they spent lots of quality time together having dinner, talking, making love and simply holding each other. Until that moment, Jordan never knew she could love a man the way she loved Dilan. Dilan rarely wanted to talk about his marital situation. Sometimes he would act as though the marriage was over and he no longer wanted to be in it and other times he would suggest that he didn't want to leave his family. Jordan was very appreciative to Dilan for all the help that he provided for her, but in some ways, she felt used. She gave her complete heart and soul to him; yet, she was only his fantasy--a place where he could escape his busy, stressful life. Jordan spent her birthday alone and weeks later a new year began--still lost, with no direction. In spite of her sadness and roller coaster of emotions toward Dilan, she continued her search for a teaching position at a high school teaching History. The hard work paid off. She only needed to take the teacher certification exam. A few weeks into January, Dilan sent an email, something he did often while traveling.

January 27, 2003

Hi Jordan,

I am frustrated because I cannot see you when I need to without putting everything that I have worked for at risk. What I mean by that is...you have become a special person in my life, but the part of my life that involves you cannot coexist with the life that I live every day. This became apparent this past Friday night. I was not able to meet you because of other commitments that I have in my everyday life. Also I am being pressured by Linda because she thinks that I am having an affair--Which is true! But her suspicion is making it difficult for me to see you as I wish and it is becoming a problem for me. It is becoming a problem for me because I do not want to disappoint you and I most certainly do not want to hurt you. I once thought that I could do this and not develop uncontrollable feelings.....but things do not go as you always want them to.

Where do we go from here? I do not know. I have a need to see you but I am not sure if you have the patience to deal with me and my circumstances; especially considering I stood you up this past weekend. Where do we go from here? I think only you can answer that question.

Dilan

Still, they continued to see each other. The passion grew more intense each moment they spent time together. Although they both had estranged spouses, (Jordan living apart from Tevin and Dilan traveling 50% of the time away from his family) the affair didn't seem wrong. It felt so right. Jordan felt that Dilan was her soul mate and that they simply had a case of "bad timing" in their lives.

February 4, 2003

Seeing you last night made my day. I did not realize just how much I missed you. It seems that being away from you somehow makes my heart grow fonder and makes me appreciate you even more. As I have always said...I think that you are a very special person that deserves so much more than you have been dealt so far. But I am sure that great things are waiting for you in the future. I am a firm believer that good things happen to good people and you are definitely a good and wonderful person.

Last night when I looked into your eyes I melted…I think you are the most sensual and sexiest lady that I have been with. Somehow you make me feel like a teenager having sex for the first time. I think I better end this email now…Good Night!

Dilan

Dilan continued to send emails during his travels. At the time, they didn't seem corny to Jordan. She was so blinded by her own thoughts of what she felt was love. Why would she put so much love and trust in a man who was cheating on his wife? And Jordan began to ask herself other questions. "Did I try hard enough to save my marriage?" "Why am I falling for a man who clearly is not committing to his family and could show that same dishonesty toward me?"

February 13, 2003

Jordan,

I always enjoy knowing that you cherish my friendship and companionship. I may not say it but you do have a special place in my mind and heart.

Jordan, you are a very special person and I look forward to spending any amount of time that I can with you. And when I am with you I am never distracted by anything else. I love the conversations that we have…I love holding

you in my arms...I love making love to you....and I espe-
cially love lying next to you feeling the warmth of your
body and the throbbing of your heart next to mine.

Jordan I do care...more than I express...more than I say!

Dilan

Jordan tried to focus on her career and she was becoming more financially independent. Dilan continued to help her as needed and often sent gifts. But after almost a year, Jordan questioned her relationship with God and wanted to build a closer relationship with God, end her affair with Dilan, and possibly seek counseling again with Tevin despite his relationship with another woman. While all these thoughts were running through her mind, Tevin finally decided to file for divorce. A part of Jordan was disappointed because she always wanted a family and it didn't seem like she would ever get to experience one of her own. Each time she tried to get thoughts of Dilan out of her head, he would contact her with his charming words. She continued to look for happiness from others instead of focusing on how she could make her life happier. She still found it difficult discovering how to simply love herself first..

June 2, 2003

Jordan,

I have to say, you are very special to me and I care for you
more than you think. All I want is to see you happy and

like I have said many times...happiness is going to be what you make it... you have to make your self happy first. I can only provide so much, Tevin can only provide so much and whoever else can only provide so much. You have to decide within yourself what makes you happy and from there try to achieve it. In the real world we know that things are not that simple, but sometimes we have to try and make them that simple. The real world also dictates that we cannot have everything that makes us happy so we have to prioritize things. We have to decide what things we can live with and those things we can live without....money, fancy cars, a loving mate, a loving friend, security...or whatever else there may be.

Jordan, I think that you are a very special and loving person and over the past year you have given me something that I could not have found anywhere else. Since I have matured I have become a seeker; I am always looking for the end of the rainbow or that missing element. This is a result of my upbringing and being so shy when I was a kid and as a young adult. When I was young I accepted the safe and secure route, which is why I married when I did and why I stayed married in the earlier years of my marriage. The reason I am married today is different...the kids. I want to be a father and raise my kids. This is my story; do not let it be yours...that is my advice. You have nothing to stop you from making your life what you want it to be.

Our relationship is one that is special to me. I enjoy every single moment that I spend with you and I am displeased when I have to leave you. When we make love it is like I am making love for the very first time because I can feel the passion that you have for me when I look into your eyes and I hope that you can feel the passion that I have for you. Even though it has been nearly a year, the excitement of knowing I am going to see you overwhelms me. I hope to see you this evening so that I can look into those beautiful brown eyes of yours.

Dilan

Jordan couldn't believe that an entire year had gone by. The divorce was almost final and Tevin and Jordan were getting along fine. She'd forgiven him for the abuse and not being a better husband to her. She was happy for his new relationship; and even though it hurt a little, she accepted the fact that he was a better man for someone else. Jordan's career was going well. She was enjoying her teaching job and began a more active role at her church. But, somehow, she still felt alone and empty. What she felt as love from and for Dilan was a temporary fix while she spent time with him. When Dilan was away, the guilt of having this type of relationship with a married man was weighing heavy on her shoulders. She realized that Tevin's wrong-doing did not justify her feelings for another man while she was still technically married. She had also justified the affair by telling herself that Dilan didn't really love his wife and was there only for the kids. So, in her mind, it seemed harmless.

Imagine yourself as each character, what would you do differently in each circumstance?

What specific advice would you give to each?

What Bible verses would help Jordan get through her trials?

_____

_____

_____

_____

_____

_____

_____

_____

_____

_____

_____

_____

_____

_____

_____

_____

_____

_____

_____

_____

_____

JACQUELINE E. PERRY

_____
_____
_____
_____
_____
_____
_____
_____
_____
_____
_____
_____
_____
_____
_____
_____
_____
_____
_____
_____
_____
_____

I FORGIVE YOU

_____

_____

_____

_____

_____

_____

_____

_____

_____

_____

_____

_____

_____

_____

_____

_____

_____

_____

_____

_____

_____

_____

_____

_____

_____

_____

JACQUELINE E. PERRY

3

The Divorce

Jordan and Tevin went to court on a Tuesday. They agreed on matters regarding joint properties and the judge granted the divorce. As they walked out of the courtroom and into the parking lot, Jordan looked at Tevin as he attempted to give her a hug. Still slightly bitter, Jordan extended her hand, as Tevin reached for a hug.

"I think a handshake will do," Jordan told Tevin.

"Wow, really? Okay, Jordan," Tevin said as he grinned and shook her hand.

She walked away, toward her car.

"Jordan!" Tevin yelled out. "I'm sorry. I hate things turned out this way. I did love you and I will still be here for you whenever you need me. It's the least I can do for the pain

I've caused you." Jordan felt some comfort after he said that.
However, she still felt somewhat lonely and sad about the
situation. At the same time, she was confident that her life
would go on.

Jordan immediately began planning a trip--alone. She
found a great deal on a trip to Cancun, Mexico. It wasn't her
first choice in places to visit, but for the price, she was will-
ing to go just to get away and relax her mind. During her
3-day trip, Jordan enjoyed relaxation and meditation. There,
she had a chance to reflect on her life and exactly what she
wanted to make of it. She was so in love with Dilan, but
she knew that things needed to change in order for her to
have a fulfilling life. On the last day in Mexico Jordan met
a few people from the East Coast, even a handsome single
guy with whom she enjoyed dinner a few hours before her
flight. His name was Bradley. He was from New England
and was attending a seminar with a few colleagues. The two
exchanged numbers, although Jordan really had no romantic
interest in him…at least not yet.

Jordan arrived in the States, not exactly ready to face reality. As crazy in love as she was, she tried avoiding Dilan
as much as possible. Avoiding was hard for her, at first. She
began intentionally to load herself down with work, church
activities and various projects. Dilan continued to confess his
love for her, continuing to make it difficult for Jordan to walk
away completely. Only a few months passed and Jordan was
back in his arms. He was slick; he knew just what to say to
keep her around. Jordan was still getting used to the fact that
she was a divorced woman now, but had no thoughts of ac-
tively dating. She didn't see Dilan as often as before; but he

came around from time to time. He was very contradictory when it came to how he felt about Jordan and the relationship. Jordan expressed to him her need to feel loved and how he made her feel whenever they spent time together.

Novemeber 13, 2003

Jordan,

I'm glad that you are feeling better!

Jordan, I think that you're a very special person and indeed you are special to me. It is unfortunate that I am who I am at this point in my life....otherwise who knows...things may have been different.

As I was saying this morning, you have to be selfish and look out for what is best for Jordan. You also have to break yourself of needing to feel loved. You are loved even if it is only your family members that love you. But you always have to love yourself first.

You are a special person and I know that good things will happen for you...so just hang in there and I am sure that everything will work out fine.

Dilan

While adjusting to life as a single woman, Jordan tried taking Dilan's advice. However, she made it clear to him that she was tired of him having his cake and eating it too. He wanted to keep his image of being this successful business man, happily married family man, loving father AND have Jordan as his escape from reality. With her, he didn't have to think about bills, a nagging wife, and the kids' extra-curricular activities. Things were easy when he was with her. Just as she enjoyed the affection and attention he showed her, he enjoyed having a listening ear, companionship, a physical relationship with no strings attached. With all of the great qualities that Jordan possessed, she could not understand why she continued this relationship with Dilan. She minimized her self-worth by not completely ending it with him, for good. Her friend, Mia, was the only one that she confided in when it came to Dilan or any relationship issues. Mia had her opinions about the whole thing, what she called "mess." Jordan had not seen Mia since her return from vacation. So, they decided to meet for lunch one Saturday. They met at one of their favorite Italian restaurants and sat outside on the patio. Weather was unseasonably warm on that day, mid-Fall. Jordan arrived a little bit early and got a table. Mia was running late as usual. Jordan ordered a glass of red wine while she waited.

"Well, hello there, missy," Mia said as she eased behind Jordan. Jordan got up and gave her a big hug.

"Missed you, girlie," Jordan told her.

"And I missed you too. So what's up; fill me in, honey!" Mia said as she rubbed her hands together, preparing herself for a juicy story.

Jordan chuckled and said, "Ummmm, where should I begin? Well, first of all, the trip was very relaxing. I tried my best not to think about the divorce, work or anything stress-ful. Annnnd....," Jordan paused.

"And what?!" Mia yelled out.

"I met a guy. No big deal."

"Girl, fill me in, fill me in!"

"Look, Mia, I said it's no big deal. His name is Bradley or Brad and we had dinner the last night I was in Cancun. I haven't returned any of his calls since I got back."

Mia gave her this you-are-crazy look and asked Jordan, "And why not? This could be a great opportunity for you to get a little practice developing a normal, healthy relationship. Even if it's just a friendship, you need to have a social life, Jordan. You don't get out much. When you were married, Tevin was the center of your life and everything revolved around him. Now it seems like your life only involves work and Dilan. I'm glad you made the effort to take the trip; I'm glad you finished school and jumpstarted your career...I'm glad about a lot of the things you accomplished. But think about how much more you can accomplish MINUS Dilan!" Mia shook her head and sighed.

Jordan told her, "Are you done preaching to me?"

"I'm only being a friend. You need to hear this." Mia grabbed Jordan's hand and began to pray, "Lord, I come to you asking for mercy on Jordan's soul. Guide her, Lord, in the right direction. Help her to make better decisions. Remove what is not of you, and bring love and peace into her heart. Help her to understand what true love is about. Forgive her for her sins. Bless her Lord, and bless us, bless our friendship. In your son, Jesus' name I pray...Amen."

Tears began to flow from both of them and they hugged each other tightly. "Everything is gonna be fine Jordan, I promise. Now let's eat!"

After lunch, Jordan drove home and worked on a few unfinished projects. Bradley called. She decided to answer. "Hello?" she answered.

"Hi, Jordan, this is Brad, ya know the guy you met in Cancun. The guy whose phone calls are never returned."

Jordan laughed and said, "Sorry, I have a lot going on these days."

"Oh, I see. Well, how about I help you escape from your worries and join me for dinner soon. Let's saaay...tomorrow night?" he asked.

"Bradley..."

He interrupted her and said, "You can call me Brad."

"Oh. Well, Brad, I don't think that's a good idea."

"Jordan, it's just dinner. I'd really enjoy your company. We had great conversations in Cancun. I haven't stopped thinking about you since then. I understand that you are recently divorced; so am I. I just want to get to know you and possibly develop a friendship and go from there. Okay?"

Jordan smiled and finally said yes. For once, Dilan was out of her mind for a few minutes. But, as soon as she finished her conversation with Brad, Dilan sent a text asking to see her later on that night. Jordan proudly ignored the text, turned her phone on silent and tossed it on the floor. Later that night before getting ready for bed, Jordan called Mia and told her about her plan to meet Brad for dinner. Of course, Mia was ecstatic about it!

"I will give you all the details of the date," Jordan said.

"Ya better not leave ANYTHING out, I want every detail," Mia said after a quick chuckle.

Jordan yawned. "Yeah, yeah, well I need to get some rest. I will talk to you tomorrow. Bye," said Jordan.

The next morning, Jordan got ready for church. She had missed a couple of Sundays, especially since she'd been on vacation. As she arrived at church, she noticed a few new faces, People were mingling and she approached the pastor and briefly talked with him.

"So, Miss Jordan, how are you?" he asked her.

"Well, I'm just fine. I'm blessed, ya know."

"Yes, indeed you are; indeed you are," he said. He continued, "I saw Tevin at the early morning service. I really want to counsel you two. You can work things out."

"Well, Pastor Harper, the divorce was finalized a couple of weeks ago," Jordan explained.

"Umm, I see. I didn't realize that. It's still not too late to restore your marriage. Services are about to start. Let's continue our conversation later. Be sure to make an appointment with Ellen (the church administrator)."

"Did I hear my name?" said Ellen as she approached the two.

"Oh, hi there," said Jordan as she gave Ellen a hug. Pastor walked away to begin the church service. "I'll check pastor's calendar and get back with you this week. Okay, hon?"

"Okay," said Jordan as she walked to the sanctuary to find a seat. The sermon was about forgiveness. Pastor Harper explained how God has a forgiving heart and how we should humbly come to him and sincerely confess our sins. Tears began to roll down Jordan's face. She knew that she wanted to run to the altar and fall to her knees. She just kept holding back. She was thinking about what others would say, instead of thinking of her own soul and how much it needed to be saved. Her inner voice kept whispering to her heart to let go and let God…let God overflow her with blessings and miracles in her life. Disobeying God, she ignored everything and remained in her seat. After service, she didn't stay to chat with anyone. She walked swiftly to her car. As soon as she got inside the car and closed the door, she began to scream at the top of her lungs, "Oh Lord, I am so sorry. Lord, I'm sorry." She cried and cried and cried. Finally she started the car and headed home. Shortly after she arrived home, Brad texted her, "Can't wait to see you. Text me your favorite restaurant and the time you wanna meet me, and I'm there."

Jordan texted him back just seconds before a call came in from Dilan. She ignored it once again. She began thinking about what the pastor said about giving the marriage another chance. Jordan started wondering if there was hope and whether or not she gave up too easily on Tevin and the marriage. Would change have taken place if Tevin received therapy for his anger? Would consistent prayer and marriage counseling be enough to restore what was never a healthy marriage? Jordan had all these thoughts and questions in her head. She considered calling Tevin one day soon to discuss a possible reconciliation, but she kept putting it on hold. It was soon time for her to get ready to meet Brad. So she tossed all those thoughts to the side and focused on enjoying her evening with Brad. As she was taking a shower, her phone rang. It was Brad leaving a voicemail saying that he was sending a driver to get her and wanted her to text her address. Jordan was impressed. She and her ex-husband had a comfortable lifestyle, but they were never over the top with spending. However, she felt it was a nice gesture and texted the address to him. Jordan was getting a little bit excited about seeing him. She chose a nice, romantic, American restaurant with a French-inspired menu and live jazz. She had been there a few times with Tevin and his colleagues and their wives. Jordan was running later. She tossed several dresses on the bed, curled her hair, then straightened it, changed jewelry a few times, changed lipsticks twice—she was a total wreck. Minutes later, the driver rang the doorbell. Jordan was still deciding what dress to wear. Even though she'd started to lose a few pounds, she wasn't completely comfortable in showing off her figure. She decided on the little black dress. She always believed that black was slimming. She opened the door and told the driver to give her just a few more minutes. He waited at the door and shortly Jordan proceeded to the front door. He escorted her to the car and opened the back door. Setting on the seat was a huge bouquet of pink, yellow and purple tropical flowers and a Cancun postcard with a note written on it that read: "The day we met was one of the best days of my life."

Jordan was smiling from ear to ear. It took about 30 minutes to arrive at the restaurant. As the driver pulled up at the front of the restaurant, Jordan noticed Brad waiting outside with his hands behind his back. He walked briskly to the car, opened the door and presented her with more flowers; this time it was pink tulips which happened to be her favorite.

"Brad, you are just too much, really!" Jordan said with a grin.

"And you are worth it and more. You can leave them in the car." They walked into the restaurant, heading toward the private dining area. Bradley reserved the entire room for them. "Wow, I'm used to being spoiled, but not this soon," said Jordan.

"The night is not over yet. This is only the beginning," explained Brad.

"What? No, I don't think I can handle all of this in one night, Brad."

After a little chit chat, they soon ordered dinner and a bottle of wine. That night, Jordan let all of her stresses go and totally indulged herself in the moment. She enjoyed every stare from him, every word he said to her, and every hug, kiss and touch from him. After dinner, Brad got in the car with Jordan.

"So, where are we headed next?" asked Jordan.

"Cove Island…"

"Oh," said Jordan. She was quiet most of the drive there. Brad held her hand the entire way. Minutes into the drive, Brad stole a kiss from her. Jordan did not back away. She melted. At that moment, in her mind she was thinking: "Dilan who? Tevin who?"

They arrived at the beach and Brad told Jordan to wait in the car. He was making sure that his surprise for her was ready. Brad walked back to the car and took Jordan by the hand. "Close your eyes," he said. They walked to the beach. Brad had candles surrounding the blanket where he had a romantic picnic set up with wine, fruit and chocolates.

"Okay, open your eyes," he told Jordan. Her mouth was wide open, in shock. She gave Brad a big hug and told him how thoughtful he was for putting all of this together. Brad and Jordan sat under the moonlight with a blanket wrapped around them. Jordan did not want the night to end. An hour later, it was time to part ways. It was a Sunday, they both had to work the next day and Jordan believed in getting plenty of rest.

"Well, it's ten o'clock. You wanna head back?" asked Brad.

"Yes, it's almost past my bedtime. But if I could have my way, I wouldn't want this night to end," said Jordan. They walked back to the car and while they were on their way to Jordan's apartment, Brad continued to tell Jordan how much he wanted to get to know her.

"We need to take things slowly," Jordan told him.

"I know, I know." They arrived at Jordan's apartment and he walked her to the door. This time, he gave her a long passionate kiss and they said their goodbyes. Jordan quickly called Mia to briefly inform her about the date. But she also let Mia know that she had to get to bed and would give her more details the next day.

The following day at school, the students noticed her glow and how her mood seemed more cheerful than usual. Faculty members also noticed the slight change in her mood. By the end of the day, that mood quickly changed. Dilan came banging on her door. Jordan opened the door.

"I just wanted to check on you and make sure everything is okay," Dilan said. "I haven't heard from you in a while. You haven't answered my calls or texts."

"Dilan, you're the one who is always talking about how I should focus on my happiness and not so much on you, since your other life that does not include me, is YOUR priority!" Jordan said, her voice rising.

"Look, I know what I said and yes I meant what I said. But at the same time, I do miss you and I want you, Jordan." "Yeah, you want me alright," she said.

"No, it's not just about the sex, Jordan. You know how much I care about you," Dilan explained.

Jordan was about to say something, but Dilan quickly began kissing her lips. Jordan gave in and that night they had intercourse. Once again, Jordan lay their dazed and confused as he got up to leave.

"See, this is what I hate. We enjoy each other, then it's over, just like that-you have to leave!" Jordan said as she started to cry.

"Baby...Didn't you enjoy your little date last night?" Dilan asked.

"What? So now you're spying on me? How did you know about that?" she asked.

"Ummm, don't worry about it...I have my ways of finding out things," said Dilan.

"Whatever, Dilan, whatever!" Jordan mumbled.

"I gotta go, alright? I gotta go," he said.

"Fine. Go!" Jordan told him. He kissed her on the forehead and Jordan walked him to the door, holding his hand; and they said goodbye. Again, Jordan was left lying across her bed, drowning herself in tears.

Imagine yourself as each character, what would you do differently in each circumstance?

What specific advice would you give to each?

What Bible verses would help Jordan get through her trials?

_____
_____
_____
_____
_____
_____
_____
_____
_____
_____
_____
_____
_____
_____
_____
_____
_____
_____
_____
_____
_____
_____

JACQUELINE E. PERRY

_____

_____

_____

_____

_____

_____

_____

_____

_____

_____

_____

_____

_____

_____

_____

_____

_____

_____

_____

_____

_____

_____

_____

_____

_____

_____

_____

_____

_____

I FORGIVE YOU

JACQUELINE E. PERRY

_____
_____
_____
_____
_____
_____
_____
_____
_____
_____
_____
_____
_____
_____
_____
_____
_____
_____
_____
_____
_____
_____
_____
_____
_____

4

The Struggle

While Jordan struggled in her personal life regarding relationships with family members, men and her spiritual life, she continued to move up in her career and education. She earned a second masters degree and applied for the position of principal at one of the local elementary schools. Weeks later, she received an offer and accepted. Three years had passed, and she was still seeing Dilan. She and Brad dated off and on, but she later found out that he was still legally married with considerations of reconciliation with his wife. Jordan began to think that she had "I date married men" written all over her. It seemed to be the only type of men she attracted. So, she just decided to deal with the Dilan situation. No matter how successful her career appeared, her self-worth was extremely low.

One afternoon after a long day at work, she began reading an email that Dilan sent on his birthday, March 4, 2005. He talked about how it had been nearly three years since they had begun sharing each other's lives and he expressed how much he wanted to come over that night to celebrate his birthday.

She truly tried to end things with Dilan months later in September, especially when she thought things would turn out differently with Brad. She sent Dilan an email expressing how much she needed to end things and he responded.

September 13, 2005

Hey Jordan,

I think of you often and if I were a single man I would not cheat as you suspect. Your email summed up our relationship. The first year everything was great and was on a good track with promises of something really special. I truly enjoyed our relationship more than you will ever know. But things changed and my attitude changed as well.

Our relationship was and is more than just sex but circumstances could not allow me to let our relationship grow further than it had. I had to back off from my feelings and not allow myself to love you more than I could afford. My life is complicated and your life is a bit more complicated than mine but in a different way.

The reality of it all is I could not allow myself to love you more because I am married which would not be a big deal but I have children that I love more than I love myself and I would die without seeing them on a daily basis. Then there is your financial situation which complicates our relationship more than I let on. It bothers me that you struggle and there is nothing I can do about it. Therefore in order to not stress myself I just do not see you as often as I would like. It is important to me to take care of those that I love and if I cannot it hurts. So not seeing you as often removes some of the stress I feel when I see you struggling as you do. But I am sure my stress level is nothing compared to yours.

Your email sounded so final and I am saddened by that. But I do understand that you have to move on. Anyway I wish you the best and I will forever have a special place in my heart for you.

Dilan

When Dilan sent the email, he didn't know about Jordan's new position, which would soon improve her financial situation. They both seemed so sure about moving on and Dilan was always contradictory in his conversations about their relationship. He would say all these things about how much his kids meant the world to him, but that same year, Jordan found clues that he was possibly seeing someone else besides her. Despite both their positions regarding why the relationship should end, they stayed together three MORE years. That next year in 2006, Jordan learned that she was pregnant. She told Tevin and Mia first. Jordan was about five weeks pregnant and was experiencing pregnancy symptoms that many pregnant women didn't experience in the first trimester.

Tevin was surprised but didn't really have a whole lot to say about it. He had clearly moved on with his life but, as always, stated that he would be there for her no matter what. Mia was disappointed, especially because of all the "preaching" she did, encouraging Jordan to get it together. She stressed that Jordan was so much better than this lousy so-called love affair.

Surprisingly, Brad called her while she was going through this pregnancy. Jordan was still unsure about when she was going to tell Dilan, and whether or not she was keeping the baby.

"Brad? So what do you want? Why are you calling me? You lied to me. You made me feel like a queen, and then I get the news that you are actually married. Why Brad, Why?" Jordan expressed her frustration.

"It was very complicated," Brad said. "I was indeed separated, not divorced. I thought I wanted to try and fix the marriage. I know I should have been upfront with you. I was confused but realized that you can't force things. She is not my soul mate; you are. I want you in my life again. I want to try this again. Can we start over, please?" Brad seemed very sincere. Jordan didn't know what to say. She didn't know if she should tell Brad about the pregnancy. She thought to herself that he would notice the slight weight gain, but he just kept looking into her eyes, waiting for an answer (They were using Skype™).

Jordan took a long, deep breath. There was silence for a moment. Then, she decided to drop the bombshell. "Talk about bad timing…I truly believe you and I wish that I could erase everything wrong in my life and start over with you. But Brad, I'm expecting," Jordan explained.

"Expecting? You mean that you're pregnant? Tell me that's not what you mean, please!"

"Yes Brad," she said quietly. Brad's eyes began to tear up. He didn't know much about Dilan and didn't ask Jordan any details. He told Jordan that he would call her later and discuss things. He really didn't know what to say. The only thing he asked was if she was keeping the baby, and Jordan told him that she wasn't sure. Brad rubbed his hands across his face in disbelief and ended the video call.

"I'll call you later," he said.

Jordan called Mia back. Mia said that she should go ahead and tell Dilan. Jordan hung up with Mia and called him. She called, hung up; called again and hung up.

Finally he called back. "Hey, what's up? Your calls kept dropping," Dilan said.

"Huh, guess I had a bad signal," Jordan lied. "Dilan, I need to tell you something."

"Okay, well shoot…"

"I've been feeling a little sick and weak lately and so I took a pregnancy test. I think I'm pregnant," she explained.

"Jordan, tell me you're joking! So if you are, you know you are not keeping that baby, right? You are not about to ruin my life, Jordan," Dilan told her.

"Dilan, I'm not sure. I've always wanted to have kids and now that I'm over 30, this is a great time to just get it out of the way. I'm not sure if I'll have this chance again. You know that I had a few miscarriages before, during my marriage. Please don't make me kill my baby, please!" she cried.

Dilan hung up the phone without saying a word and rushed over to Jordan's apartment. Dilan arrived at her apartment and began banging on the door insistently. Jordan would not open the door. He kept banging on the door and calling for about 15 minutes straight. He finally left and called back shortly after. Jordan answered the phone.

Dilan simply said "If you think you are going to ruin my life, you have another thing coming. You will regret keeping this baby. It's in your best interest NOT to have this baby."

Dilan hung up and Jordan cried and cried until she fell asleep across the bed. After a few days of no contact with Dilan, things cooled off. They talked and Dilan decided to join her at her first doctor's appointment since taking the pregnancy test. She was about six weeks along in her pregnancy. The nurse provided the two with several options. They needed to make a decision soon because Dilan had really gotten to Jordan. She was afraid that he would snap and do something crazy to her. So, after leaving the doctor's office, they went to Jordan's place and discussed their options. They agreed on having a medical abortion, a procedure that was fairly new at the time. They read over the pamphlets that explained how the procedure would take place.

Jordan started paraphrasing the statements to Dilan," "So, I would go into the clinic and the doctor will administer a pill, some type of hormone that stops the pregnancy. Then the next day I will take a pill that will induce labor. But it has to be done by the seventh week, I think. Dilan we don't have much time. I'll need to schedule an appointment. Are you coming with me?" "Of course I will," he said. Jordan cried in his arms.

Days before the appointment, Jordan called Dilan and talked to him about how much she was against going through with it, especially since she had an abortion as a teenager. It was extremely emotional and painful for her to have to deal with this again. Jordan was feeling sick that entire day and called Tevin to come over because she was having a hard time reaching anyone, even Dilan. Tevin immediately rushed over to her apartment. Jordan opened the door. Tevin began to tell her that he needed to talk to her about something very important. Before he could finish a sentence, Jordan felt light-headed and her cramps became more intense. She rushed to the bathroom. She was having a miscarriage. Shortly, Tevin hurried to get her to the E.R. Tevin stayed with her there for a few hours until they finally released her later that night. Tevin drove her back and walked her inside and into the bedroom. Jordan, for a moment, felt warm and fuzzy and thought for a split second that maybe they could have worked things out.

"So what was it that you were trying to tell me earlier?" Jordan asked.

"Uh, uh…this is not the right time; we'll talk soon, okay?" Tevin mumbled.

Jordan gave him a puzzled look and said, "Fine." She was experiencing mixed emotions about the miscarriage and about attempting to end the pregnancy. Deep down she wanted to have the baby and wondered if God was giving her a sign to get out of the situation with Dilan and try to work it out with her ex-husband. Tevin placed a couple of bottles of water on the nightstand, warmed her a bowl of soup and asked if she needed anything else before he left. Jordan replied no and walked behind him to lock up.

"Take care of yourself," he said. The phone kept ringing most of the night. Jordan finally turned it on silent. She cried and cried. Then she prayed: "Heavenly Father, heal my body and soul. Protect me. Guide me and deliver me from evil, Lord. Give me strength to walk away from situations that are not in my best interest. Help me to make better decisions. Where I am weak, make me strong. In your son, Jesus' name I pray. Amen." Soon after, Jordan fell asleep.

The next morning Jordan felt renewed. She'd slept better than she had in a long time. She picked up her phone and noticed that she missed dozens of calls, mostly from Dilan. He still didn't know about the miscarriage and he was probably on his way over. It was about 9:00 am when Jordan woke up and the appointment was for 11:00 am. Jordan listened to one of the voicemails that he left: "You'd better NOT be changing your mind on me. I will be there around 10:15." Jordan didn't bother about calling him.

Once he arrived there, Jordan immediately told him, "Dilan! I lost the baby! I had a miscarriage. So I hope you are happy. I hope your selfish ass is happy. You got your way. You're safe now. You will continue to have your 'pretend' family and live happily ever after."

Dilan had a look of surprise on his face. "I AM sorry Jordan. It's not that I'm being selfish, but I also want you to live a better life. You are doing so well with your new position…Yeah, I found out about that and I'm hurt that you didn't share such a big accomplishment with me. But, anyway, as I was saying…I don't want a baby to interrupt your life or cause confusion in my own situation. I love you, Jordan. I care about you more than you will ever know," he said. Dilan grabbed Jordan and hugged her tightly for a while, holding back tears. "Well, I gotta go," Dilan said. He stormed out the door and didn't look back.

Jordan took a few days off from work and rested. Her sister called about her mother's surprise birthday party in Alabama. Jordan wasn't ready to explain her situation but told her sister that she would try to make it down there. Later, she noticed an email that Dilan sent a few days earlier:

April 3, 2006

Hey Jordan,

I really hate putting you through this and it did not make me happy. More than anything I did not want to cause you any pain or anguish and I especially did not want to change the person that you are. However in these types of situations, I have learned that you have to keep to your normal life's routine. Also you have to trust in God and ask him for forgiveness and have the faith that he is a forgiving God as the scriptures say. That is what I have done and is what I did a long time ago. If we dwell on it then the devil will tear at your soul and cause you to lose faith. So do not dwell on this and let's move on with our lives but remember not to make the same mistake again.

Having said that, I will always have a special connection with you no matter how long I live. Actually I would not like for our friendship to end even if our love affair does. So go to your mother's party and never let them know this part of your life because no matter what, all will judge but none have to bear your burden. That is the natural order of life and that is the natural process of growing up. Perhaps it is easy for me because I have always been a secretive person and have always bore my burdens alone. This was a burden for me not only because I have never felt this bad about anything; but I have never felt this bad about what I have put someone through. I hope that you are able to visit your mother, and that you enjoy yourself.

Dilan

Despite all of the things Dilan said, the two still stayed together until 2008. During those last two years, Dilan started spending a little more time with her. He did experience some guilt about Jordan having to go through the miscarriage. He also felt bad about asking her to have an abortion. Each day he came by the school to take her to lunch. They continued the relationship and Jordan seemed content, even though she knew it was wrong. She felt like such a hypocrite. She maintained her roles in the church, thinking this could make up for her wrong doings. In her mind, no one could help who they loved. Realistically, she knew that the moment she put herself in that situation, nothing positive would come out of it—only temporary satisfaction. She sometimes thought about Brad and texted him about the miscarriage, but he never responded. Educated, successful career, beautiful, giving, strong—in spite of all these qualities, Jordan was insecure. Instead of focusing on her relationship with God as she desired, she focused on other desires—desires to have companionship from any man who gave her attention. And that man happened to be Dilan, a married man. So why? Why would Jordan risk so much to be with someone like Dilan when she could have any decent man that was available. She had this feeling for him that she just couldn't explain. In May of 2008, just a few months before the affair ended, Jordan felt a little distance from Dilan, more than he had been before. She asked if there was someone else and he said no. In hindsight, she started to think about clues that may have been indications that he was seeing another woman, besides his wife, that is.

One night before Jordan got ready for bed, Tevin called. He was calling to finally tell Jordan about the important news.

"Hello?"

"Jordan, how are you?"

"I'm fine. What's up?"

With no hesitation, Tevin told her, "Well, I'm getting married."

Jordan was speechless. She hung up the phone and something clicked in her head at that moment that it was time to get out of that so-called relationship with Dilan. Later that night, she sent an email to his wife confessing everything. She didn't intend to send the email; at the time it just felt good to get everything out. It was like her therapy. However, Jordan actually ended up sending the email. Jordan had so many emotions swarming around in her head. Minutes later, she received a reply responding mostly to Jordan's statement about how she really was a good person. Jordan began skimming through the email and the part that stood out the most was, "Good people don't sleep with a woman's husband..." It hit her! All the good things, in her mind, outweighed this mistake with Dilan. Then she thought, "But how can this be a mistake when I continued this affair over and over for years?" Jordan reached for her Bible, read a few scriptures and prayed. She remembered learning in Bible study how no sin is greater than another-a sin is a sin and it separates us from God. "Lord, I repent. Forgive me Lord, forgive me," she cried out.

She woke up the next morning with a sense of relief. Everything was now out. Had she told Dilan's wife, Linda, about the affair for the wrong reason? Well, partly, because she felt he may have been seeing someone else; she was glad that it was out. Her intent was not to break up the marriage at all. Later, Dilan's wife, Linda, and Jordan would create a bond neither would ever imagine. Jordan saved Linda from what could have been 20 more years of deceit, lies and disrespect--a marriage that was unreal.

Now, in 2008, Linda kicked Dilan out of the house the next day. He called Jordan and surprisingly he was not very upset. Dilan admitted to seeing another woman named Charlotte. While Jordan was finally ready to move on with her life without Dilan, she was devastated. It was weird, she admitted, to be nonchalant about him being married but felt so heartbroken over the other woman. Dilan also told Charlotte about Jordan. Once he did that, a turn of crazy events began to unfold. Jordan was confused at this point, more than she had ever been. She was in so much pain, emotionally and she could only imagine the pain that Dilan's wife was feeling. Linda emailed Jordan her phone number and asked her to call later that day. Linda wanted more details about the relationship that Jordan and Dilan shared. Jordan called her later that night; it was her last day off in an attempt to recover from all the stress of the miscarriage. Jordan could not comprehend how unbelievably calm Linda was when hearing Jordan give all these details about when, where, why and how! Linda mentioned that she found out about Charlotte a few days prior to her sending the email and thought that was the reason Jordan decided to confess and end the affair. But Linda did not confront Dilan about Charlotte until after she read Jordan's email.

Dilan claimed he loved Charlotte and wanted to spend his life with her. Jordan found that hard to believe since he spent quite a bit of time with her during the 6-year affair and he was very supportive, especially during her financial instability. After the hour-long conversation with Linda, Jordan sent Dilan an email with about 20 reasons why she knew that he indeed did love her. Jordan felt that her pain was God's way of showing how deeply hurt he was for her role in this mess. Now that Dilan had moved out of the house, he did miss being there with his children and stopped by daily after work to visit. He moved in with Charlotte, a possessive, insecure woman whose main goal was to ruin anyone's life who could possibly interfere with her being with Dilan. She read the email that Jordan sent and continued snooping through Dilan's emails, text messages and calls. Jordan was angry about the entire situation and hated herself for allowing Satan to control her emotions. There were so many opportunities to walk away before any of these events could take place.

Charlotte began sending threatening calls and text messages even though Dilan claimed to be crazy in love with her. Later Linda and Jordan would find out just how crazy in love he was. While Charlotte was busy making sure Dilan's marriage was ending, Linda forgave Jordan. She could understand that Jordan was going through a difficult time in her life after her divorce. Linda did not excuse the behavior but empathized with Jordan and felt that she truly was sincere in her apology regarding her part in the affair. Linda also realized that Dilan had a way of charming others, and his manipulative ways could perhaps make it hard to walk away. In spite of all the craziness with Charlotte and Dilan, Jordan remained cordial with Dilan but was worried about this unhealthy relationship with Charlotte. He told her that he felt that he was in love with all three of them and had gotten caught up. Dilan, although successful and powerful in a business sense, possessed much insecurity. He felt the need to feel loved by women. He had charm and wealth, but was short and not very attractive. But his best qualities stood out and he used those to get the attention that he wanted. The attention from his wife was not enough.

At first, Jordan had a hard time moving on and Charlotte could definitely sense that. For a while the phone calls and threats became overwhelming for Jordan. She was not accustomed to this type of drama. Dealing with Dilan's situation was enough. Jordan needed to focus on her career as an educator and not let nonsense from Dilan's "other" mistress distract her from her goals. Months went by and Jordan and Linda became closer. Linda was very hurt, and so was Jordan. They consoled each other, as weird as that may sound. At times, it seemed like Linda was the mistress and Jordan was the wife. Linda gave Jordan encouraging words. Jordan could not believe how strong Linda was being. Jordan began to think to herself, "Here I am, crying over Dilan to his own wife. How selfish of me. I should be comforting her and showing her my remorse for what I did."

For whatever reason, Linda felt a genuine affection for Jordan and continued to tell her how much she forgave her. Jordan and Linda continued to communicate and check on each other from time to time, with plans to meet some day for lunch.

JACQUELINE E. PERRY

Imagine yourself as each character, what would you do differently in each circumstance?

What specific advice would you give to each?

What Bible verses would help Jordan get through her trials?

_____

_____

_____

_____

_____

_____

_____

_____

_____

_____

_____

_____

_____

_____

_____

_____

_____

_____

_____

_____

_____

_____

_____

JACQUELINE E. PERRY

5

The Transition

While Jordan had indeed moved on, she occasionally met Dilan for lunch. Her good pal, Mia, felt that she should leave him alone altogether. Eventually, Jordan took Mia's advice and declined all of Dilan's invites to lunch. However, she did respond to his "hello" text messages. She heard from Linda stories about Dilan and Charlotte. Dilan and his girlfriend fought a lot. She sliced his clothes and set his bright red Porsche, that he loved dearly, on fire in front of the house where Linda and the children lived. Charlotte even called the police on Dilan a few times when they argued. Now, Dilan has a misdemeanor on his record and ended up staying in jail overnight on several occasions. It was just a complete mess. Jordan couldn't believe that Dilan would put himself in this situation. She was so glad to have her life back, completely back! No drama whatsoever.

After a couple of years, Dilan and Linda finally divorced, which left him almost broke. But Jordan certainly felt that he deserved it after all the pain he caused. He misled all three women. Although when they were together, Jordan knew that he was still legally married to Linda and playing the role of husband, he gave her the impression that he truly loved her and she fell for his trap. With all of these years of waiting…Jordan lost a lot of her life. Eventually she became a strong, successful woman, but it took a lot of pain and life lessons to get there.

Linda called Jordan and was finally ready to officially meet after this ordeal. They had not seen each other, besides a few times when Jordan worked at the radio station. So, Linda wanted to celebrate her new beginning. The divorce was final and she was also ready to move on. Dilan played games with her as if he wanted to make the marriage work, but would always go back to Charlotte, who was conniving and manipulative— same characteristics as Dilan. Even though Jordan and Linda talked several times, Jordan was extremely nervous about seeing her for the first time after the affair ended. Jordan arrived at the restaurant early. She thought she'd need a few drinks first. She called Mia to help calm her nerves as she waited. "Oh, she's coming," Jordan told Mia.

"Ok, good luck," Mia said. Linda came up to the table and greeted her with open arms. They both drowned themselves in tears. All Jordan could say was, "I'm sorry, I'm so sorry."

She said it over and over and over again. Linda looked her straight in the eyes and said, "I told you, Jordan, I forgive you, I mean that."

Then she slapped her. Jordan was in shock. She was hesitant for a second and said, "You know, I deserved that; "I played a role in the affair and I was wrong."

Then Linda cried some more and gave her another hug. The impulse to slap her was part of her frustration and pain, even though Charlotte was the one creating most of the pain and had a major role in breaking up the family. They briefly discussed the past and basically dogged Dilan and Charlotte. They felt that they were both helpless souls.

Jordan felt a weight lifted off her shoulders. Although she knew Linda had already forgiven her, it still felt good to see her in person and feel the power of her forgiveness.

"Dilan is not a good role model for our kids," Linda said. "He's going down the wrong path. He's putting his life at risk, his position at the radio station at risk, everything, just to be with that woman. And that kills me."

She told Jordan that she has nothing to do with him. She changed her number and blocked him from calling. He can only reach her through email. He contacts the kids directly. "So, let's toast to a new beginning and no more drama; and most of all no more Dilan. Wooohooo!" screamed Linda. They laughed and with their pinky fingers made a pact to never discuss Dilan, ever.

"By the way, so how are things with you and your ex?" Linda asked.

"Well, ya know he's getting married; and I received an invitation," said Jordan.

"Wow! Are you gonna go?"

"I'm not sure yet." The ladies chatted for a little while longer and decided to wrap things up and they both agreed that they would meet again in the near future.

Jordan relaxed later that evening. It was a Saturday night and she decided to stay in and get some rest. The next morning, she got ready for church. She came to the altar that Sunday and asked for prayer. Jordan knew that God had forgiven her, but she just needed that extra comfort because she was still weak. The pain she experienced from Dilan and Tevin caused her to feel as if she was not good enough to be in a normal, loving, healthy relationship. Even after Dilan, she dated a few men and some were married, and Jordan was not trying to go down that road again. So, she continued to pray and pray and pray. She soon decided to become celibate and focus more on her position at school and her relationship with God. It felt good to have her life back. Her friendship with Tevin was better than ever. He was happy that she forgave him, and continued to keep in contact with her until his wedding day. Jordan often thought how things could have been with the two of them. She wished that she could have seen that change in him while they were together. But she realized that sometimes, things are not meant to be and maybe it took the ending of their marriage for him to make that change. Jordan decided to attend the wedding. Many of his family members didn't exactly greet her with kindness as she walked into the wedding. His mother and brother felt that she was wrong for leaving him. Tevin's father, however, was always kind to her and he gave her a hug before walking inside the church where the wedding was held. She felt awkward as she walked the aisle looking for a seat. Thoughts continued to run through her mind because she didn't know how she would feel watching him and his bride exchange vows. It was a small wedding with probably less than 100 people there. The groom and best man entered. Tevin noticed Jordan sitting in the third pew and gave her a wink. She smiled and waved. The ceremony began, and Jordan remained calm. She realized that life was certainly going on and she wanted so much for "Mr. Right Now" to find her. After the wedding, she decided not to attend the reception. Jordan arrived at her place and flopped on the sofa. It was an emotional weekend for her. Nonetheless, she was prepared for a new chapter in her life.

Imagine yourself as each character, what would you do differently in each circumstance?

What specific advice would you give to each?

What Bible verses would help Jordan get through her trials?

JACQUELINE E. PERRY

I FORGIVE YOU

JACQUELINE E. PERRY

_____

_____

_____

_____

_____

_____

_____

_____

_____

_____

_____

_____

_____

_____

_____

_____

_____

_____

_____

_____

_____

_____

_____

_____

_____

_____

_____

6

Starting Over

Jordan continued focusing on work and less drama. She kept herself drowned in work, attending workshops, administrators' conferences, luncheons and meetings. At last, she had a weekend to do nothing but relax. Out of the blue, Brad gave her a call. They had not spoken since she told him she was pregnant. She never had the chance to tell him that she miscarried.

"Hello?" he said. "So, how are things with you, Jordan?" Jordan paused for a second. She was shocked to hear from him.

"Actually, I'm doing just fine. How about you?"

Brad told her "Things are going well, dealing with less stress--now that the divorce is final. I'm involved in church, reading the Bible more, traveling…Life is good. So how's the baby?"

Jordan chuckled for a moment, but with a tad of sadness, she explained to him that she miscarried.

"What? Oh, Jordan, I'm so sorry, babe." With a sense of relief, Brad had the courage to ask Jordan to be in his life again. He told her that although he was angry and confused, he never stopped loving her. He thought about her every single day they were apart. "Jordan, I'm not saying that I'm happy that you didn't have the child, but do you know what this means for us? We have a chance. You're not seeing him or anyone else are you?"

"No, of course not," Jordan replied.

"I never stopped loving you," Brad told her. Jordan insisted that they take things slowly. She wanted to make sure this relationship would last. For months, they rebuilt their friendship and got to know each other all over again. Brad even began going to church with Jordan very often. Overall her life was turning around. The elimination of many of those negative factors greatly increased her happiness level.

She completely removed Dilan from her life, but he continued to call from time to time. She knew how miserable he was but felt no sympathy for him. Jordan finally changed her number, but often heard stories from Linda whenever they would talk. Linda told her that things were still crazy with Dilan and the girlfriend, Charlotte. Linda was stuck in the situation because she wanted Dilan to continue to have a good relationship with his kids. Linda later learned that the so-called grandson, a toddler that Charlotte was raising with Dilan was actually their child. Drama after drama, after drama continued.

Jordan was thinking, "Didn't we promise never to discuss that loser again?"

One day, Jordan decided to call her just to see how Linda was feeling, hoping not to hear more about the mess of Dilan and Charlotte.

"Hey Linda?"

"Well, hello, Miss Jordan! How the heck are ya?"

"Well, things are great with me," Jordan said. "Brad and I are in a good place. All the drama in my life is non-existent and I have a better relationship with God. I am truly blessed. I have been through hell and back and I don't want to go back to that place where I once lived…hell on earth."

"I'm glad things are great for you. But I know how you don't like talking about Dilan and crazy woman," Linda paused for a moment and took a deep breath and continued. "Dilan shot himself yesterday. Apparently he could no longer handle the stress that he was going through. I won't get into details but he and that woman had a love-hate relationship and it was starting to affect me and the kids," she explained.

"Wow, well, I feel bad for the kids," Jordan said. She really didn't know what else to say. "Oh, and I imagine that Charlotte has probably lost it, she was literally crazy over him."

"Yeah, but ya know what? I'd bet anything she will move on pretty quickly and find some other man to obsess over," Linda said with a slight grin. "He did email me his suicide note and I showed detectives. He basically apologized for all of his affairs, and…," Linda explained as Jordan interrupted her.

"Huh, gotta go Linda, we'll be in touch again soon, okay?" Jordan hung up and was a little in shock; although she didn't wish death on him, she felt some relief. To Jordan, his death permanently symbolized that this chapter of her life was over and never to be repeated.

Minutes later, she called Mia and was about to tell her the news. "Hey Mia, guess what?"

"Wait, wait, hold that thought…I am already on my way over there," Mia said.

"What? You are on your way over here unannounced?"

Mia laughed and said, "No, I'm telling you now…On my way, bye!"

Jordan just shook her head and said to herself, "Goodness, that Mia is somethin' else. I meant uninvited."

About half an hour later, Mia came knocking on Jordan's door. Mia hugged Jordan and jumped right into it: "So, what's the news?" she asked as she rubbed her hands together.

"It's not exactly good news or anything. Dilan killed himself," Jordan explained.

Mia's eyes were wide and mouth wide open. "That's not good news? Are you kidding me?"

"Mia! Please have some dignity here. The man did a lot of wrong to a lot of people; but we are Christians here, right? I don't exactly have a lot of respect for him or any respect for that matter, but I feel bad for the kids. And since he killed himself, he doesn't have that chance of repenting, so I do feel bad for him as well."

"Okay, I hear ya. But the guy was still a jerk," Mia said, rolling her eyes.

"You know what? Mia, you are a piece of work; you really are…," said Jordan. The two sat around and chatted a while longer and later left to do a little shopping and visit the nail salon. They hadn't spent much time together since Jordan began devoting most of her spare time to Brad. Later, Mia dropped Jordan off back at her place.

Jordan asked, "Are you coming back in?"

"No, I'm gonna head back. The hubby and I are having date night. We got a babysitter! Woohoo!" Mia yelled.

"Cool! Brad has plans for us tonight. He's being all secretive about it. I guess he's surprising me or something. Who knows?"

The two waved goodbye and Jordan walked into her apartment. But before she opened the door, she noticed her favorite flowers setting on the doorstep with a note. "Get ready, I'll be there around 8:30. Love, Brad."

Jordan smiled and went inside. She rested for a few minutes, wondering what Brad had up his sleeve this time. She began getting ready. When Brad came to pick her up, he blindfolded her. Jordan was beginning to feel like he was recreating their very first date. In some ways, he did; there was just one detail added. Later in the evening, after leaving the restaurant, Brad instructed Jordan to put the blind-fold on again. So, she did. When they arrived at the beach, Brad removed the blind-fold, got on one knee and grabbed Jordan by the hand. "Jordan, we haven't been together for years and years, but I know you are the one I want to spend the rest of my life with. You allowed me to become a better person. You opened my eyes and now I see things that I didn't see before. Because of you, I love more; because of you, I care more; because of you I have a closer relationship with God; because of you, I give more. Jordan I can go on and on and on. All I know for sure is that I want you as my wife. You are like my best friend and I cannot imagine my life without you in it. Jordan Maria Velasquez will you do the honor of being my wife?"

Brad gave a long sigh as he waited for Jordan's answer. She was in shock. She did not expect this to happen so soon, especially since they agreed recently to take things slowly. Jordan said a quick prayer and felt in her heart that everything was fine. Sometimes it is okay to live in the moment and follow your heart. Without a doubt, she knew that saying yes was the right decision. "Well?" Brad asked.

"YES, YES, YES! I WILL MARRY YOU, BRADLEY MARTIN PHILLIPS!!!!"

Brad picked her up, swinging her around. They both were enjoying their moment of pure bliss. She was going to mention to Brad about Dilan's death, but didn't want to ruin the evening by bringing up his name. Days later, she received a call from Linda about the funeral. Attending her ex-husband's wedding was enough for Jordan. She declined and moved on completely.

Six months later, Jordan and Brad married on that very beach where they had their first date and proposal. A few close friends and family attended. Honeymoon was spent in Bora Bora. Linda moved back to the Virgin Islands where she grew up and spent time teaching yoga. She was very much into the natural way of life. She was a free-spirit and had a kind heart. Not many women will forgive as willingly as she did with Jordan. Sadly, one of her kids died in a car accident and the older two were off to college in Florida. Charlotte, just as Linda predicted, fell in love with an older man and caused chaos in his life. But the old man loved chaos and married her.

Brad and Jordan later found out that they conceived a child during their honeymoon. While this was not how they wanted to spend the early part of their marriage, they were still very happy.

Imagine yourself as each character, what would you do differently in each circumstance?

What specific advice would you give to each?

What Bible verses would help Jordan get through her trials?

_____

_____

_____

_____

_____

_____

_____

_____

_____

_____

_____

_____

_____

_____

_____

_____

_____

_____

_____

JACQUELINE E. PERRY

JACQUELINE E. PERRY

John 14:27 *Peace I leave with you, my peace I give unto you: not as the world giveth, give I unto you. Let not your heart be troubled, neither let it be afraid.*